Merlin, Morgan Le Fay and the Magic of Camelot

Children's Arthurian Folk Tales

BABY PROFESSOR

EDUCATION KIDS

Speedy Publishing LLC

40 E. Main St. #1156

Newark, DE 19711

www.speedypublishing.com

Copyright 2016

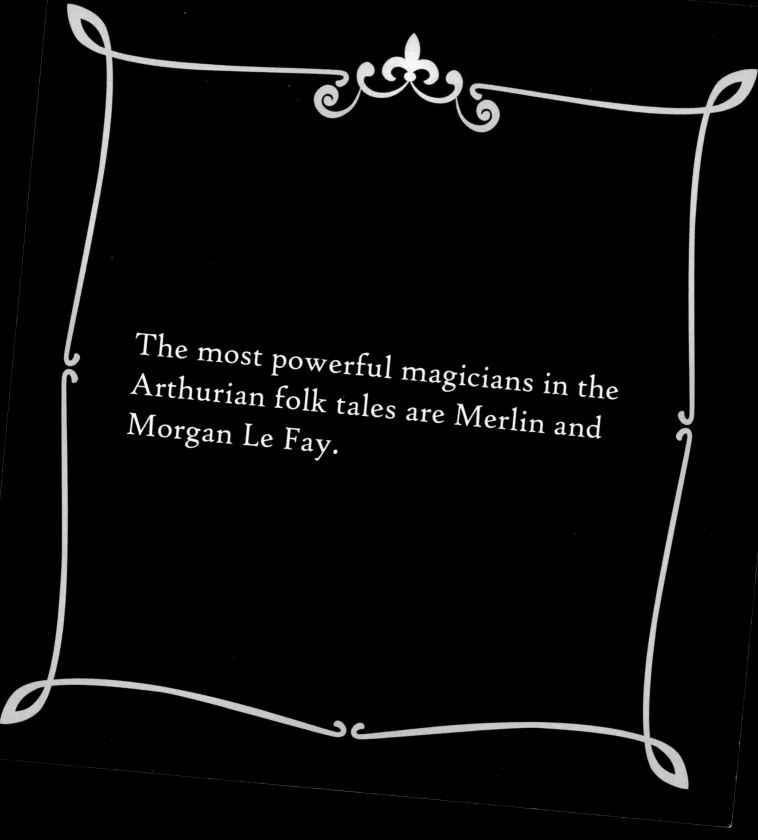

The most powerful magicians in the Arthurian folk tales are Merlin and Morgan Le Fay.

Merlin the Magician

In the legends of King Arthur, Merlin was a powerful wizard who helped and advised the king. He was Arthur's adviser, a prophet and a magician.

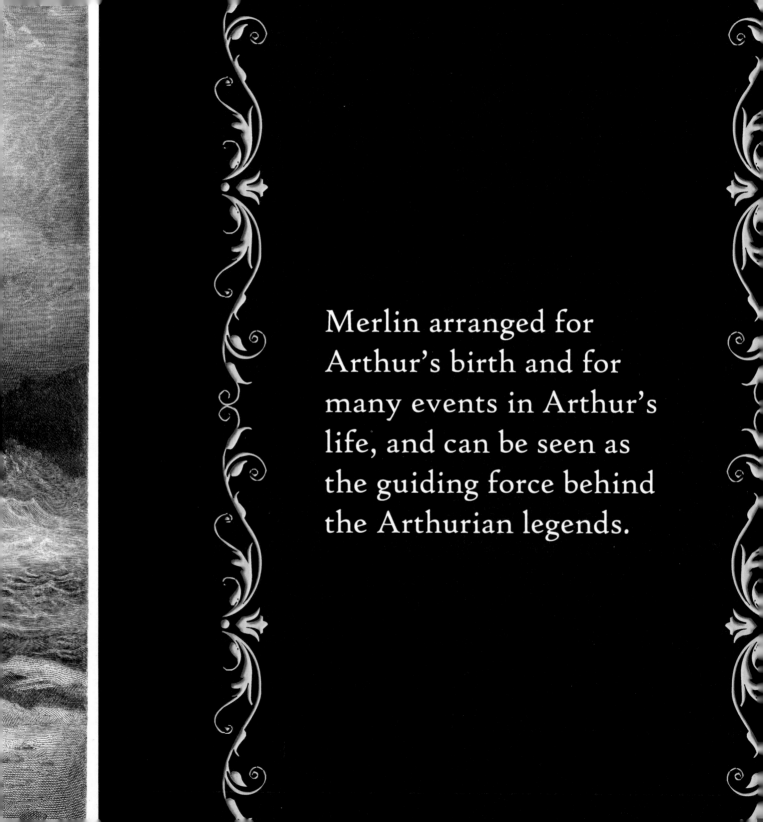

Merlin arranged for Arthur's birth and for many events in Arthur's life, and can be seen as the guiding force behind the Arthurian legends.

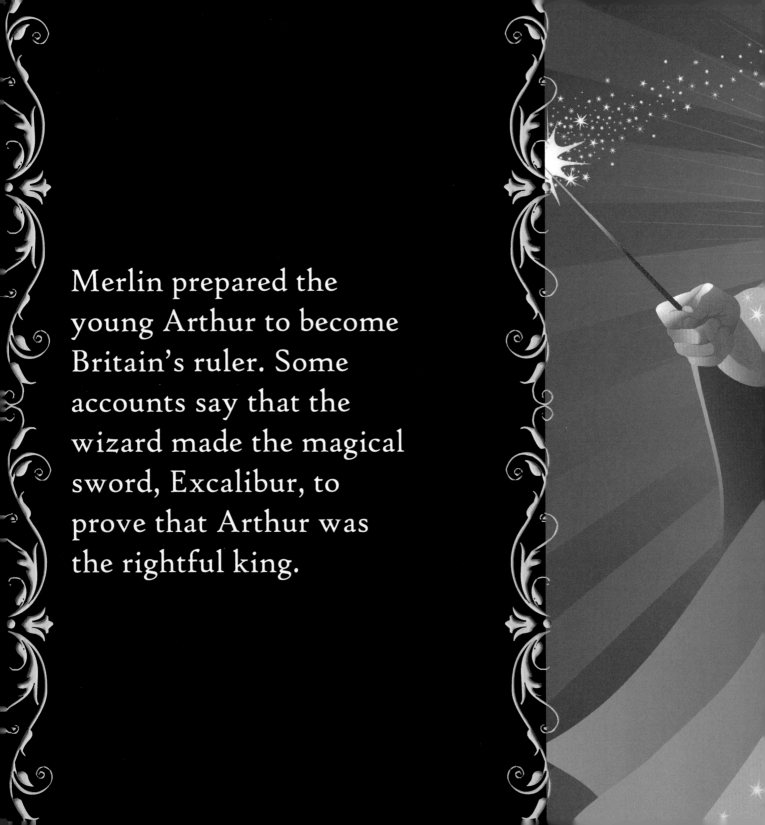

Merlin prepared the young Arthur to become Britain's ruler. Some accounts say that the wizard made the magical sword, Excalibur, to prove that Arthur was the rightful king.

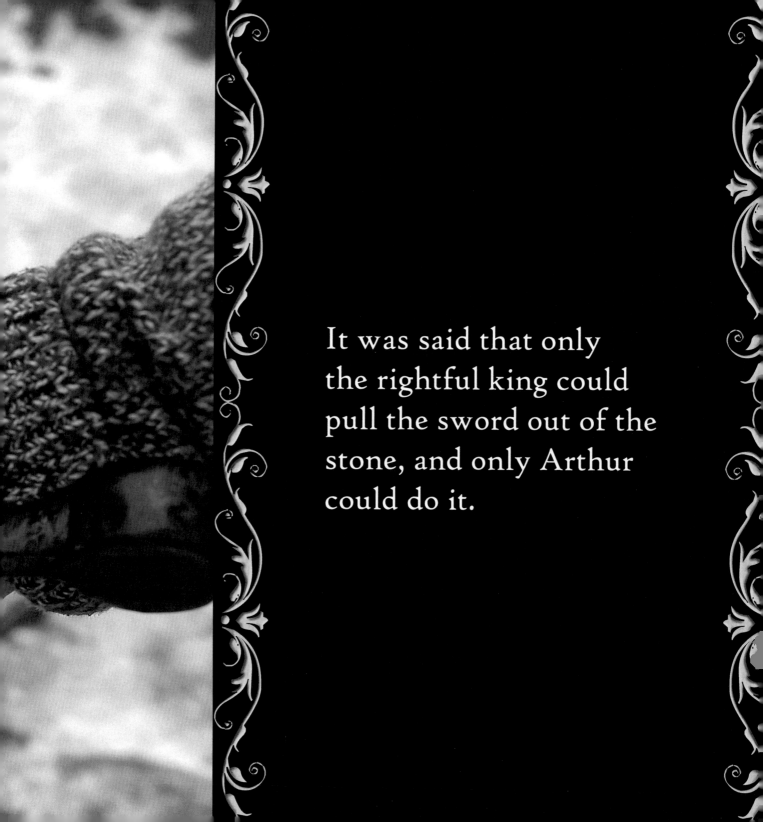

It was said that only
the rightful king could
pull the sword out of the
stone, and only Arthur
could do it.

When Arthur became the king, King Arthur made Merlin his trusted helper and adviser.

According to other stories, it was Merlin who created the Round Table around which Arthur and his knights gathered to plan and to discuss the welfare of Camelot.

He was Arthur's helper and adviser in many things. However even Merlin, with his great powers, could not prevent the final crumbling of Arthur and the knights' fellowship.

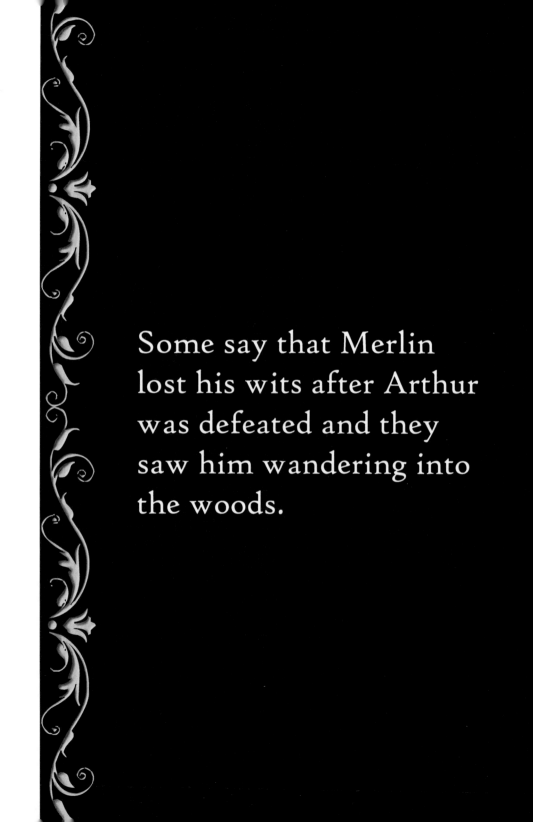

Some say that Merlin
lost his wits after Arthur
was defeated and they
saw him wandering into
the woods.

However, in most versions of the story, Merlin was tricked by a witch named Nimuë, sometimes known as the Lady of the Lake, with whom he had fallen in love.

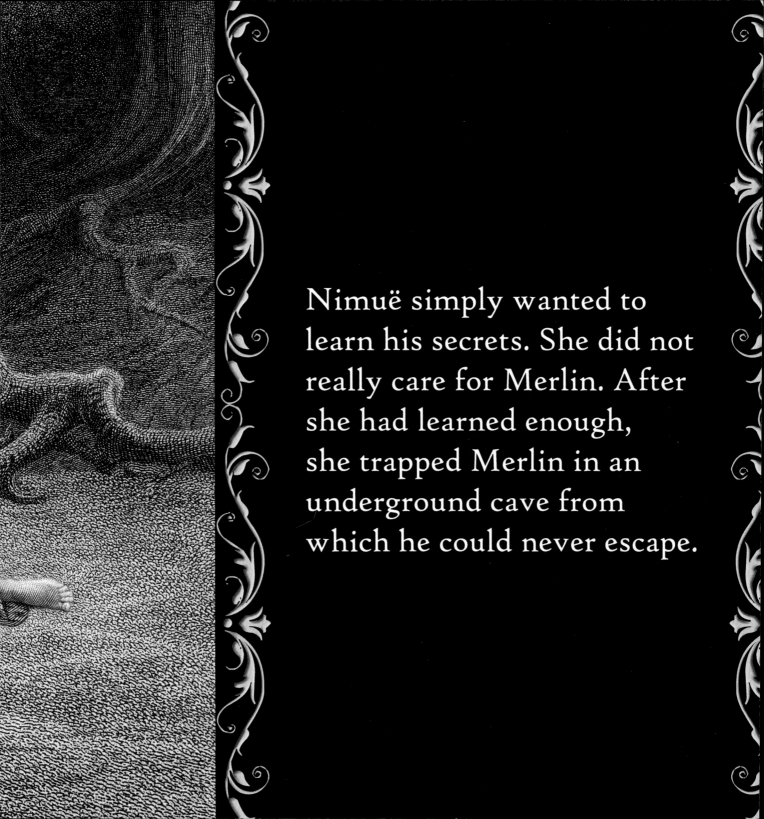

Nimuë simply wanted to learn his secrets. She did not really care for Merlin. After she had learned enough, she trapped Merlin in an underground cave from which he could never escape.

MORGAN LE FAY

Morgan le Fay, in most versions of the stories, is Arthur's half-sister. Some writers say Arthur and Morgan had a son named Mordred.

However most writers say that Mordred's mother was Arthur's other half-sister, Morgause, who was older than Morgan.

Morgan le Fay was responsible for Gawain's adventure with the Green Knight. She had given the Green Knight the ability to survive after having had his head cut off.

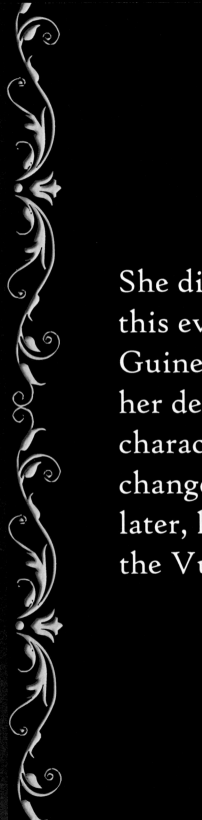

She did this in hope that this event could frighten Guinevere, or even cause her death. Morgan's character began to change in stories written later, like "Tristan" and the Vulgate Cycle.

These stories made
her a mortal enemy of
King Arthur and Queen
Guinevere. She became
more sinister and later
writers give her a wicked
and evil character.

Morgan fell in love with a young knight who happened to be Queen Guinevere's cousin. The knight and Morgan were lovers until the time that Guinevere heard of it.

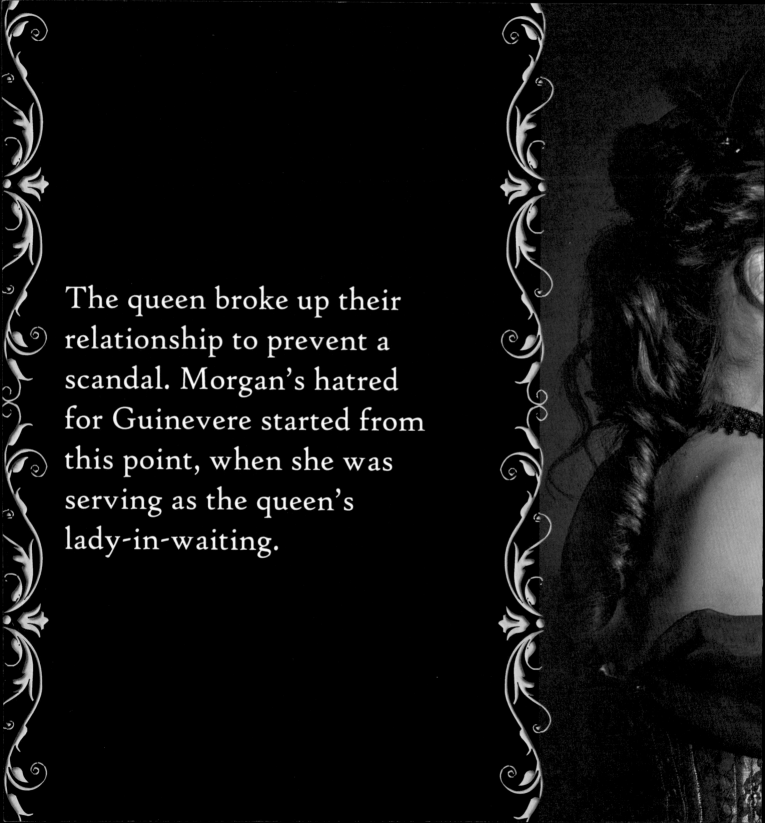

The queen broke up their relationship to prevent a scandal. Morgan's hatred for Guinevere started from this point, when she was serving as the queen's lady-in-waiting.

Morgan never forgave Guinevere and she sought revenge upon the queen. With her vengeful spirit, she went in search of Merlin to learn magic. She offered to love the sorcerer in exchange.

Visit

BABY PROFESSOR
EDUCATION KIDS

www.BabyProfessorBooks.com

to download Free Baby Professor eBooks
and view our catalog of new and exciting
Children's Books

Made in the USA
Columbia, SC
24 February 2019